W9-CTI-488

NEW MEXICO

Rennay Craats

www.av2books.com

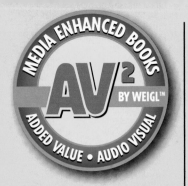

AV² provides enriched content that supplements and complements this book. Weigl's AV² books strive to create inspired learning and engage young minds in a total learning experience.

Your AV² Media Enhanced books come alive with...

Audio
Listen to sections of the book read aloud.

Key Words
Study vocabulary, and complete a matching word activity.

Video
Watch informative video clips.

Quizzes
Test your knowledge.

Go to **www.av2books.com,** and enter this book's unique code.

BOOK CODE

V 9 6 3 4 8 4

Embedded Weblinks
Gain additional information for research.

Slide Show
View images and captions, and prepare a presentation.

AV² by Weigl brings you media enhanced books that support active learning.

Try This!
Complete activities and hands-on experiments.

... and much, much more!

Published by AV² by Weigl
350 5th Avenue, 59th Floor
New York, NY 10118
Website: www.av2books.com

Library of Congress Cataloging-in-Publication Data
Names: Craats, Rennay, author.
Title: New Mexico : the Land of Enchantment / Rennay Craats.
Description: New York, NY : AV2 by Weigl, [2016] | Series: Discover America |
  Includes index.
Identifiers: LCCN 2015048011 (print) | LCCN 2015048330 (ebook) | ISBN
  9781489649089 (hard cover : alk. paper) | ISBN 9781489649096 (soft cover :
  alk. paper) | ISBN 9781489649102 (Multi-User eBook)
Subjects: LCSH: New Mexico--Juvenile literature.
Classification: LCC F796.3 .C733 2012 (print) | LCC F796.3 (ebook) | DDC 978.9--dc23
LC record available at http://lccn.loc.gov/2015048011

Printed in the United States of America, in Brainerd, Minnesota
1 2 3 4 5 6 7 8 9 20 19 18 17 16

082016
210716

Project Coordinator Heather Kissock
Art Director Terry Paulhus

Photo Credits
Every reasonable effort has been made to trace ownership and to obtain permission to reprint copyright material. The publisher would be pleased to have any errors or omissions brought to their attention so that they may be corrected in subsequent printings. The publisher acknowledges Getty Images, iStock Images, and Alamy as its primary image suppliers for this title.

NEW MEXICO

Contents

STATE TREE
Pinyon

STATE BIRD
Road Runner

STATE ANIMAL
Black Bear

STATE FLAG
New Mexico

STATE FLOWER
Yucca Flower

STATE SEAL
New Mexico

Nickname
The Land of Enchantment

Motto
Crescit Eundo
(It Grows as It Goes)

Song
"O Fair New Mexico," words
and music by Elizabeth Garret

Population
(2014Census) 2,085,572
Ranked 36th state

Entered the Union
January 6, 1912, as the 47th state

Capital
Santa Fe

Discover New Mexico

S cenic beauty and a rich cultural mix are two of the primary attractions in New Mexico. Nicknamed the Land of Enchantment, New Mexico has beautiful landscapes that enchant residents and visitors alike. The scenery varies from snowcapped mountains to scorching deserts. The state's culture is a fascinating blend of Native American, Hispanic, and European influences. New Mexico's Folk Arts Program helps preserve the traditional arts of these cultural groups. A program called the Arts Trails supports practicing artists, who take inspiration from the state's heritage and natural wonders.

Along the Rio Grande, visitors can travel parts of El Camino Real, which means "The King's Highway." This roadway dates back to the late 1500s and was the first of its kind built by the Spanish in what is now the United States. Santa Fe, which means "Holy Faith" in Spanish, is one of the oldest U.S. towns. It was founded in 1610, a decade before the Pilgrims landed at Plymouth Rock. Today, some of the most sophisticated research facilities in the world are found in New Mexico. In 1945, the first atomic bomb was completed and tested in the state, after which scientists continued to conduct research in the fields of nuclear energy and space exploration.

The Land

Covering an area of **121,590 square miles**, New Mexico is the **fifth-largest** state in the country.

New Mexico's highest mountain is **Wheeler Peak**, at **13,161 feet**.

The Acoma Pueblo people built Sky City in the thirteenth century, making the city more than 800 years old. It is still inhabited today.

Beginnings

Evidence of humans living in the area of New Mexico dates back 11,000 years. Pueblo Native Americans were the main native group encountered by Europeans who explored the area in the 1500s. The Pueblo people lived primarily along the major rivers, such as the Rio Grande and the Pecos.

Conquistadors from Spain were the first Europeans to explore the area. The Spanish set up a colony and maintained control of the region from the mid 1500s to the late 1600s. The United States did not gain control of the area that would become New Mexico until the end of the Mexican-American War in 1848.

It was not until the railroad made its way into the state in the late 1800s that New Mexico saw any major population booms. The Santa Fe Railroad finally crossed into the territory in 1878, eventually stretching into Santa Fe in 1880. Along with the railroad, many homesteaders from other areas of the United States moved to the territory. By 1910, the population of New Mexico had reached 195,000.

Where is
NEW MEXICO?

New Mexico has nearly 60,000 miles of highways. Interstates 10, 25, and 40 comprise approximately 1,000 miles of these roads. The state's 26 Scenic **Byways** range from 4 to more than 600 miles long. A commuter rail line called the New Mexico Rail Runner runs north and south in the middle of the state.

ARIZONA

United States Map

New Mexico

Alaska   Hawai'i

MAP LEGEND

- New Mexico
- ☆ Capital City
- ● Major City
- ▲ Aztec Ruins Monument
- — Rio Grande
- ☐ Bordering States
- Mexico
- ☐ Water

MEXICO

1 Santa Fe

When the U.S. Territory of New Mexico was established, Santa Fe was already its capital city. The city retained this status even after New Mexico became a state. Today, visitors can experience the city's many museums and art galleries.

2 Albuquerque

New Mexico's largest city is Albuquerque. The city was founded in 1706 and has a rich history that combines Pueblo culture with Spanish influence. In its early days, it was an important trading city. More recently, Albuquerque has become a hub of military and technology research.

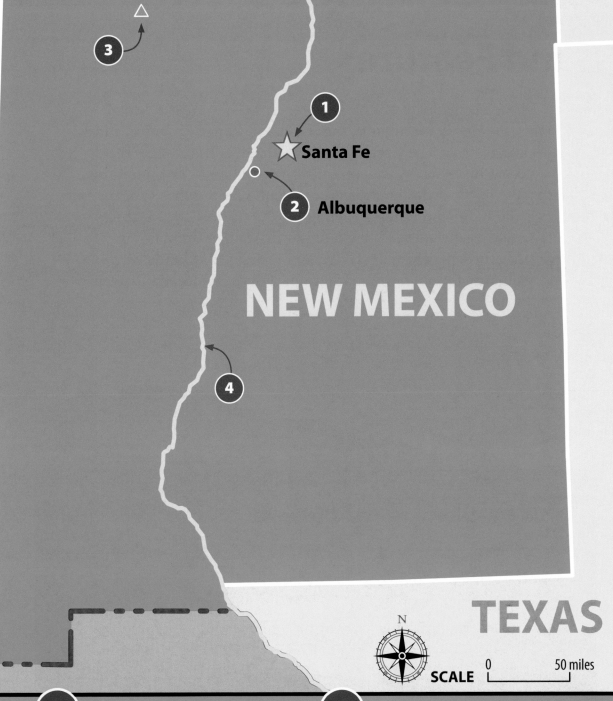

3 Santa Fe

1 Santa Fe

★ **Santa Fe**

2 **Albuquerque**

NEW MEXICO

4

TEXAS

N

SCALE 0 ⊢————⊣ 50 miles

3 Aztec Ruins Monument

The Aztec Ruins Monument was actually built by ancestors of the Pueblos, not the Aztecs. The National Monument is home to the ruins of multi-storied buildings called "great houses" that the ancient peoples constructed. Today, the site teaches people about the lives of its ancient inhabitants.

4 Rio Grande

The Rio Grande is the fifth-longest river in North America. In addition to forming the border between Texas and Mexico, it runs through New Mexico for about 470 miles. Since ancient times, irrigation has been used to water crops along the Rio Grande, making the area suitable for farming.

Land Features

New Mexico is made up of four land regions. They are the Great Plains, the Rocky Mountains, the Basin and Range Province, and the Colorado Plateau. The Great Plains, which cover the eastern third of the state, are dissected by canyons and rivers. The Rocky Mountains run along the north-central region around Santa Fe. Southwest of the Rockies is the Basin and Range Province. The southwest area features mountains and deep valleys. The Colorado Plateau, in the state's northwest, features plains, valleys, cliffs, and **mesas**. **Badlands** with dry lava plains are found in the southern part of the Colorado Plateau.

Valley of Fire

The rock formations in the Valley of Fire are ancient lava flows. Much of New Mexico's landscape was formed by volcanic activity, and various forms of volcanic rock are found in the state.

White Sands National Monument

The white sands of the White Sands National Monument cover 275 square miles. The sand dunes at the monument move from 5 to 40 feet per year.

Rio Chama

The Rio Chama was designated a Wild and Scenic River by the U.S. Congress. The Chama, Jemez, Puerco, Conchos, and Pecos rivers are all **tributaries** of the Rio Grande within New Mexico.

Bosque del Apache

Bosque del Apache National Wildlife Refuge is popular with birdwatchers. Each winter, tens of thousands of birds gather in the wetlands.

Climate

New Mexico's climate is exceptionally sunny and dry throughout the year. The state's average annual temperature is about 64° Fahrenheit in the southeast and 40°F in the northern mountains. The average annual precipitation in Santa Fe is roughly 14 inches per year. However, averages can be misleading. There can be large differences in precipitation in New Mexico's desert and mountain regions.

Average Annual Precipitation Across New Mexico

The amount of rainfall recorded at different weather stations in New Mexico can vary widely. What features of New Mexico's geography do you think contribute to this variation?

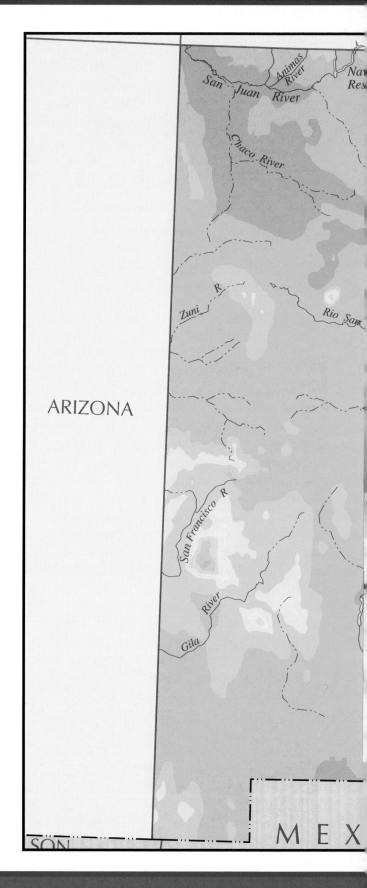

LEGEND

Average Annual Precipitation (in inches) 1961–1990

200 – 100.1

100 – 25.1

25 – 5 and less

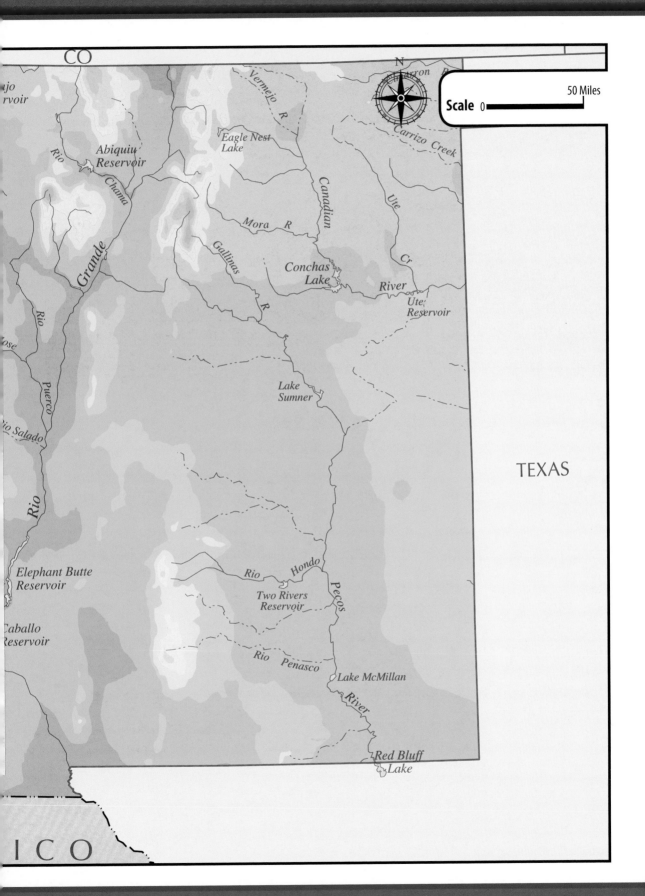

CO

Vermejo R.

N

rvoir

Rio Chama

Abiquiu
Reservoir

Eagle Nest
Lake

Carrizo Creek

Rio Grande

Mora   R.

Canadian

Ute

Gallinas

Conchas
Lake

Cr.

River

Ute
Reservoir

R.

Rio

Rio Puerco

o Salado

Lake
Sumner

TEXAS

ose

Rio

Elephant Butte
Reservoir

Rio   Hondo

Two Rivers
Reservoir

Pecos

Caballo
Reservoir

Rio   Penasco

Lake McMillan

River

Red Bluff
Lake

ICO

Mined oil and natural gas account for half of the revenue made from the state's natural resources.

Nature's Resources

Natural gas, oil, and coal are among the state's valuable natural resources. The production of natural gas, oil, and coal employs thousands of people in the state. Most oil production occurs in southeastern New Mexico. Coal is found in northern New Mexico, most notably in the San Juan Basin and the Raton Basin. Most of the state's natural gas production also takes place in the San Juan Basin. Solar power has also become an important energy source.

Copper is New Mexico's most valuable nonfuel mineral. The copper industry is located primarily in southwestern New Mexico. The state also has uranium reserves. Other important minerals produced in the state include perlite and potash. In addition, gold, molybdenum, and silver are mined.

The Rio Grande crosses the entire length of the state, flowing from north to south. Although the Rio Grande is not very deep, its water is used to **irrigate** crops along the river valley. Water is scarce in New Mexico. Most of New Mexico's lakes are actually **reservoirs**. The largest lake in the state is the Elephant Butte Reservoir, which was created by damming the Rio Grande.

The Chino mine near Santa Rita, New Mexico, is the state's largest copper mine and one of the largest open pit copper mines in the world.

Water is not only a valuable resource, but a vital necessity in an arid climate such as New Mexico's. Reservoirs such as Elephant Butte Lake ensure the state has a constant supply of water.

Vegetation

Gila National Forest, one of the largest national forests in the United States, covers 3.3 million acres in New Mexico. Apache-Sitgreaves, Carson, Cibola, Coronado, Lincoln, and Santa Fe national forests also beautify the state. Many plants, such as the creosote bush, the desert marigold, the desert zinnia, and the sunset cactus, grow in New Mexico.

The state's official flower, the yucca, grows in dry areas. The yucca looks like a pincushion of sharp leaves with a tall stalk growing out of it. In the spring, white flowers bloom from the end of the stalk. Native Americans called the plant soapweed because the roots could be used to create hair tonic and soap. They also used yucca leaves to make rope, baskets, and even sandals. The pointed leaf tips were used as needles for sewing. The sharp leaves also earned the plant the nickname "Spanish bayonet."

Yucca

The yucca was selected by the state's schoolchildren as the state flower and officially adopted on March 14, 1927.

Poppies

Poppies dot the Florida Mountains with bright colors. Florida is Spanish for "feast of flowers."

Juniper

Three-fourths of the state is covered by deep-green juniper shrubs, low pines, and prairie grasses. These plants grow well at elevations of about 4,000 feet to 7,000 feet.

Pinyon Pine

The cones of pinyon pines produce large, edible pine nuts. Native Americans were the first people to harvest pine nuts in the region.

Wildlife

Elk, deer, sheep, and porcupines live in forested parts of the state. The desert areas are home to jackrabbits, coyotes, and javelinas, which look like large boars. The Mexican wolf was once a common sight, but this type of wolf became endangered when its population dwindled to about 200. Fearing that the wolf would become extinct, conservationists worked to reestablish the animal in nature. In 1998, they began to release wolves into federally protected areas of land, and many of these animals now roam in New Mexico's Gila National Forest.

Smaller and more abundant is the tarantula hawk wasp, the state's official insect. This metallic-blue wasp feeds on the nectar of flowers such as the milkweed, but it stalks more dangerous prey to feed its offspring. The wasp paralyzes tarantulas and uses the spiders as food for its developing **larvae**.

Mexican Long-nosed Bat

The Mexican long-nosed bat lives in New Mexico but is on the list of endangered animals in the United States. The bats eat only at night.

Coyote

Coyotes roaming New Mexico's plains are able to move at speeds of 35 to 40 miles per hour. Their speed makes them powerful predators.

Roadrunner

The roadrunner, New Mexico's official bird, can run at speeds greater than 15 miles per hour. The roadrunner is also known by its Spanish name, *el correcaminos*. Its diet consists of insects, lizards, and snakes.

Javelina

The javelina is also known as the collared peccary. It is the only pig-like animal that is native to the United States and found in nature. The javelina has poor eyesight but excellent hearing.

Economy

Bandelier National Monument

Bandelier National Monument is more than 33,000 acres of volcanic landscapes. A museum, camping areas, and hiking trails are all available to visitors.

Tourism

Millions of people travel to New Mexico every year to experience its many recreational, historical, and geographical wonders. Santa Fe is the primary destination for visitors. It is located in the beautiful Sangre de Cristo Mountains and is known for its Spanish and Native American art. Many galleries can be found along Canyon Road, its main street. The city also has the Georgia O'Keeffe Museum, which displays paintings created by O'Keeffe, a famous artist who lived and worked in New Mexico for many years.

The supernatural also draws tourists. Some people believe that Roswell, in the southeast, was the site of an alien spacecraft crash in 1947. Today, the city is the location of the International UFO Museum and Research Center.

Carlsbad Caverns

Carlsbad Caverns National Park contains more than 100 limestone caves, many of which tourists can explore.

International UFO Museum

The International UFO Museum and Research Center is devoted to **phenomena** concerning unidentified flying object, or UFO, sightings and landings in the U.S.

Museum of Space History

The New Mexico Museum of Space History is located in Alamogordo. In addition to the space exhibits, the site features the International Space Hall of Fame.

Sandia National Laboratories works closely with the United States Department of Energy. It researches and develops many different kinds of energy, including nuclear and other renewable sources.

Primary Industries

New Mexicans work in printing and publishing, electronics, and stone and glass production. As in other states, service industries such as health care employ the most people. The state is renowned, however, for high-technology industries. One important high-technology facility is Sandia National Laboratories. Owned by the federal government, Sandia has operated in Albuquerque since the late 1940s. Over the years, this company has developed and tested rockets and weapons as well as conducted safety research for the nuclear energy industry.

About 50 miles west of Socorro are 27 enormous, dish-shaped antennae known as the Very Large Array, or VLA. The **antennae** form a type of telescope that receives radio waves from distant galaxies. The information received by each of the dishes is combined to create a more complete view of the universe. Each antenna is 82 feet wide and weighs 230 tons.

The Los Alamos National Laboratory employs more than **11,000 scientists** to develop new technologies.

New Mexico's **largest** employer is the University of New Mexico. It employs about **12,000 people**.

Value of Goods and Services (in Millions of Dollars)

Several major industries are grouped together in some economic categories. Mining alone accounts for 10 percent of the state's economy, which is higher than in most other states. Why is mining especially important to New Mexico's people and economy?

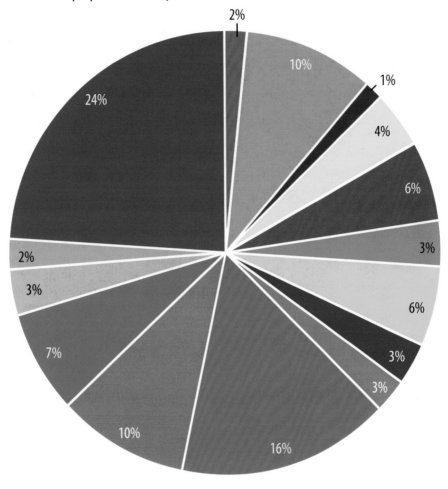

Agriculture, Forestry, and Fishing................... $1,582	Information.. $2,513
Mining $9,069	Finance, Insurance, and Real Estate $14,513
Utilities $1,325	Professional and Business Services $8,881
Construction $3,655	Education, Health and Social Services $6,797
Manufacturing... $5,531	Recreation and Accommodations................... $3,204
Wholesale Trade.. $3,012	Other Services.. $1,976
Retail Trade $5,418	Government... $21,822
Transportation and Warehousing.................. $2,587	

New Mexico is world-renowned for its chili peppers. The vegetable brings in more than $460 million to the state.

Goods and Services

Manufacturing, mining, construction, and agriculture are four traditional industries that account for close to one-fifth of New Mexico's economy. The rest of its economy is made up of the service sector. Trade, banking, insurance, and real estate are the biggest money-making services. Goods and services provided by federal, state, and local governments account for more than $15 billion of New Mexico's annual economy.

Although not as important to the state's economy as it once was, agriculture employs about 27,000 New Mexicans. Another 84,000 residents work in food processing. Meat from beef cattle and milk from dairy cows are top agricultural products. Eggs and poultry are also important. Hay, pecans, onions, and chili peppers are the state's leading crops. Farmers also raise greenhouse and nursery items, such as trees for landscaping.

Albuquerque is New Mexico's major manufacturing center. Food and beverage manufacturers, such as cereal and tortilla makers, have been expanding in recent years. Furniture companies, such as mattress maker Tempur-Pedic, have relocated to the state. Electronics producers remain the largest manufacturing employers in the state. Producers of semiconductors, silicon, and other wafers used in computers do business in New Mexico, as do producers of electronics parts. Honeywell International manufactures military communication systems and other products.

Some of New Mexico's most popular processed food products are regional favorites, such as chilies, salsa, barbeque sauces, and tortillas.

Space products are also a valuable part of the goods-producing sector. The government funds several top research laboratories, throughout the state. It also funds military bases involved in space research.

New Mexico, especially Albuquerque, is home to many technology companies. This includes Skorpios Technologies, which researches new ways of sending and receiving information.

Many of the Pueblo's villages were a collection of multi-story structures made from adobe brick. Adobe brick is made from wet mud and other organic materials that are then allowed to dry into a certain shape.

Native Americans

Archaeologists have found stone spearheads that indicate that the prehistoric people of New Mexico hunted mammoths and bison. The Cochise were among the first Native American cultures that developed in the desert areas of western New Mexico. The group existed between 9,000 and 2,000 years ago. For food, the Cochise gathered edible plants and hunted. Over time, they also learned to farm.

About 2,200 years ago, the hunter-gatherers of the Mogollon culture settled in the southwestern part of New Mexico. They lived in small villages and likely raised plants for food. The Mogollon were the first people to make pottery in the Southwest.

Another hunter-gatherer group, the Ancestral Puebloans, sometimes called the Anasazi, lived in northwestern New Mexico. They built multistoried cliff dwellings, but abandoned them in the late 1200s, probably because of a severe drought. The Pueblo Indians of modern New Mexico are their descendants. The word *pueblo* is Spanish for "village" or "town." The Pueblo groups include the Zuni, the Acoma, and the Laguna.

During the 1400s the Navajo and the Apache settled in what is now New Mexico. The Apache spread out over eastern and southern New Mexico. The Navajo settled west of the Pueblo.

Traditional Pueblo clothing included items made from cotton and leather. Skins, from animals such as rabbits or deer, were also used to create robes.

Exploring the Land

The first Europeans to visit New Mexico were Spaniards searching for cities of gold. After being shipwrecked off the Texas coast in 1528, the Spaniard Álvar Núñez Cabeza de Vaca and three other survivors spent the next eight years wandering through what is now the southwestern United States and northern Mexico. During their journey, they encountered Native Americans who told them about a kingdom of riches located farther north. Upon his return to Europe, Núñez wrote about his shipwreck and the stories he had heard about the kingdom, which came to be known as the Seven Golden Cities of Cíbola.

Timeline of Settlement

1539 Marcos de Niza, a priest, and his guide, Estéban, reach what is now New Mexico. They had been sent to scout the location of the Seven Cities.

1540 The Spanish explorer Francisco Vázquez de Coronado leads an **expedition** to the area.

1563 Francisco de Ibarra, another Spaniard, arrives, looking for gold.

1536 Spaniard Álvar Núñez Cabeza de Vaca and companions are rescued after wandering the region following a shipwreck. They begin spreading rumors they heard from the Native Americans, about a kingdom of riches called the Seven Golden Cities.

First Settlements

1598 Juan de Oñate founds the first European settlement and is named the governor of the Province of New Mexico.

Early Exploration

After the Núñez story became known, Spanish leaders planned an expedition to find the Golden Cities. A priest named Marcos de Niza was sent in advance, with a guide named Estéban. The guide was a survivor of the Núñez group. In 1539, the scouts entered what is now New Mexico. The priest saw a large Zuni settlement from the distance and returned with exaggerated tales of its grandeur. In 1540, the explorer Francisco Vázquez de Coronado traveled to the area to find the promised riches. He found nothing but the mud buildings of the Zuni Pueblo.

1821 After the Mexican War of Independence, the Province of New Mexico becomes part of Mexico.

1848 Following the Mexican-American War, the land that is now New Mexico becomes part of the United States.

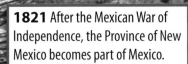
Changes of Control

Territory and Statehood

1680 The Pueblo Indians begin a major uprising against the Spanish. The Spanish work to retake control of the area for more than a decade.

1850 The New Mexico Territory is established. It includes most of what is now Arizona. In 1863, the territory is divided, and the Territory of Arizona is created.

1608 At about this time, Santa Fe is established. In 1610, it is named the provincial capital.

1912 The U.S. Congress passes a measure to admit New Mexico to the Union. President William Howard Taft makes New Mexico's statehood official.

The Santa Fe Trail was an important link between the United States and the newly independent Mexico. It was used as a trade network for 20 years. In the mid-1840s, the United States used it to invade Mexico during the Mexican-American War.

The First Settlers

In 1598, Juan de Oñate led 400 Spanish settlers north from what is now Mexico, then called New Spain. They ended up in northern New Mexico at San Gabriel, where the Rio Grande and Chama Rivers meet. The Acoma Pueblo revolted against the newcomers in late 1598. In retaliation, the Spanish killed hundreds of the Acoma.

Unrest continued, and the Pueblo burned Santa Fe in 1680. This was known as the Pueblo Rebellion. The Spanish did not reestablish their authority in the area until more than a decade later.

Santa Fe became the center of Spanish settlement in the north, and Albuquerque was the population center in the south. As the 1800s began, New Mexico had more people than Texas and California, and all three areas were controlled by Spain. In 1821, Mexico won its independence from Spain, and these lands came under Mexican rule. That same year, Captain William Becknell of the United States opened the Santa Fe Trail to transport goods 900 miles between Independence, Missouri, and Santa Fe, New Mexico.

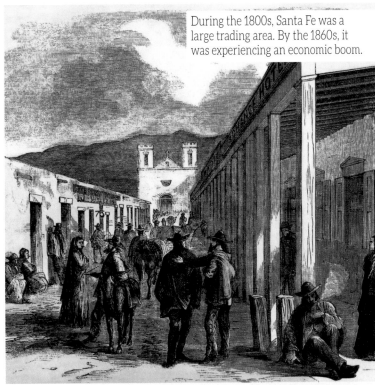

During the 1800s, Santa Fe was a large trading area. By the 1860s, it was experiencing an economic boom.

In 1846, war began between the United States and Mexico. Under the Treaty of Guadalupe Hidalgo, which ended the war in 1848, New Mexico became part of the United States. In 1850, the U.S. government established the New Mexico Territory. As the territory grew, it began to attract the cowboys, miners, railroad workers, gamblers, and cattle **rustlers** who settled this new U.S. frontier.

President James Polk acquired much of what would become Texas, Arizona, California, Utah, and New Mexico during the Mexican-American War.

History Makers

New Mexico is the birthplace or adopted home of many U.S. business leaders, such as Conrad Hilton, who established the Hilton Hotels chain, and Jeff Bezos, founder of Amazon.com. New Mexicans have served as ground-breaking politicians, activists, and astronauts.

Dennis Chavez (1888–1962)

Dennis Chavez was born in Los Chaves, in what was then the New Mexico Territory. He had to quit school in eighth grade to help support his family. Over time, however, he earned a law degree. A Democrat, he began serving in the state legislature in 1923. In 1936, he became the first Hispanic American elected to the U.S. Senate, where he served until his death.

Clinton Presba Anderson (1895–1975)

Clinton Presba Anderson moved to New Mexico when he became seriously ill with tuberculosis. Anderson's first political position was as New Mexico's state treasurer. He later served in the U.S. House of Representatives, as secretary of agriculture, and in the U.S. Senate.

Joseph Manuel Montoya (1915–1978)

When elected to the New Mexico House of Representatives in 1936, Joseph Montoya was 21 years old, the youngest person to ever have won that office. In 1940, when Montoya began service as a state senator, he was the youngest to serve in the state senate. He later went to Washington, D.C., serving in both the U.S. House of Representatives and in the U.S. Senate.

Dolores Huerta (1930–)

Dolores Huerta was born in Dawson, New Mexico, in 1930. She started her activism career fighting for the civil rights of immigrants who work as farm laborers. In 1960, Huerta created the Agricultural Workers Association (AWA) and then the United Farm Workers (UFW). These organizations ensure the rights and working conditions of farm laborers and immigrants.

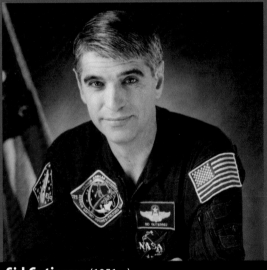

Sid Gutierrez (1951–)

Born in Albuquerque, Sid Gutierrez was the first Hispanic American to both pilot and command a U.S. space shuttle. Before joining NASA, he served in the U.S. Air Force. He was inducted into the International Space Hall of Fame in 1995.

Culture

Native American groups in New Mexico, such as the Zuni, strive to preserve their traditional culture. They do this through celebrations of traditional dances, costumes, and language.

Thanks to Spain's long-time presence in New Mexico, much of the state's culture and many of its people are of Hispanic ancestry.

The People Today

New Mexico ranks 36th among the states in total population. At the time of the 2010 Census, it had about 2 million residents, with most living in urban areas. Due to its historical ties and **proximity** to Mexico, about 47 percent of New Mexicans claim Hispanic origins. This is much higher than the same category in the country's population as a whole. The United States population is approximately 17 percent Hispanic American. About 10 percent of the New Mexico's population is Native American, much higher than the national figure of about 2 percent. Many Native Americans live on reservations in the central and northwestern parts of the state.

From **1950** to **2010**, the state's population growth has been **above the national average**.

Q What are some of the factors that have helped New Mexico grow more rapidly than many other states?

Called the Roundhouse, the New Mexico state capitol is modeled after the Zia Sun Temple. The Zia are a Native American group and a branch of the Pueblo people.

State Government

New Mexico's constitution has been in place since 1911, although it has been amended many times since then. Amendments and bills are proposed by either the Senate or the House of Representatives in the state's legislative branch of government, which meets in the capitol. If a bill is approved by a majority of the 42 senators and 70 representatives, it is sent to the governor to make into law. If the governor **vetoes** the bill, the legislative branch can still pass it if enough members vote for it again.

The governor heads the executive branch of the government. This branch develops policies and plans for the state's future. The governor also appoints many important state officials.

The judicial branch of New Mexico's government ensures that the state's laws are followed. It consists of several types of courts. The highest court in New Mexico is the Supreme Court. The next highest court is the Court of Appeals, and there are 13 district courts, 54 magistrate courts, and various lower courts.

When she was sworn in as governor in 2011, Susana Martinez became the first Hispanic woman governor in the United States.

New Mexico's state song is
"O, Fair New Mexico."

Under a sky of azure,
Where balmy breezes blow, Kissed by the
golden sunshine, Is Nuevo Mejico.
Land of the Montezuma, With fiery
hearts aglow, Land of the deeds historic,
Is Nuevo Mejico.
O, Fair New Mexico,
We love, we love you so,
Our hearts with pride o'reflow, No
matter where we go.
O, Fair New Mexico,
We love, we love you so,
The grandest state to know New Mexico.

* excerpted

The New Mexico state capitol is the only round capitol building in the United States.

Important Mexican holidays are celebrated annually throughout the state, such as *Dia de los Muertos*, or "Day of the Dead."

Celebrating Culture

Most Hispanic Americans who live in the state speak Spanish. There are many Spanish-language newspapers and TV and radio programs. Hispanic Americans celebrate their culture in New Mexico with a variety of festivals and events. The Spanish Market, for example, gives Hispanic American craftspeople a chance to showcase their art. It is held in Santa Fe twice yearly, in summer and winter. Each September, the Santa Fe Fiesta celebrates Hispanic American culture with dances, concerts, and parades.

New Mexico has 19 Pueblo Indian villages. Taos Pueblo is a National Historic Landmark and a World Heritage Site. Zuni Pueblo is the state's largest and most populous Pueblo site.

Some of the ceremonies and festivals held in the pueblos are longstanding traditions. Zuni Pueblo holds the Shalako ceremony in winter. During the ceremony, people dressed as **kachinas** enter the village and perform **rituals** to bring rain, a bountiful harvest, and good fortune in the coming year. Pueblo feast days are celebrated throughout the state. San Geronimo Feast Day at Taos Pueblo features traditional dancing as well as a trade fair displaying drums, pottery, and clothing.

Many of the state's Native Americans celebrate their culture with festivals and ceremonies. Navajo craft traditions, such as the making of turquoise jewelry and woven rugs, have been passed down from generation to generation. Every August, Gallup hosts the Inter-Tribal Indian Ceremonial. This popular event features powwows, rodeo events, arts, and a parade.

Each year, Gallup hosts the Inter-Tribal Indian Ceremonial. The event features traditional dance, music, and crafts from many different Native American groups in the area.

Since the early 1800s, the Zuni have been known for their crafts. These include jewelry made from local materials such as turquoise.

Georgia O'Keeffe's art focuses on flowers, skylines, and landscapes. She has been called the mother of the style known as American modernism.

Arts and Entertainment

New Mexico's unique landscape and culture have long influenced writers and artists. In the 1920s, the acclaimed British novelist D. H. Lawrence lived outside Taos, writing *The Plumed Serpent*. Perhaps the most noted U.S. author associated with New Mexico is Willa Cather. Her 1927 novel *Death Comes to the Archbishop* is a study of Roman Catholic missionaries in New Mexico. The author Tony Hillerman lived in New Mexico as a young man. His mystery novels, such as *A Thief of Time*, explore Navajo traditions.

Among visual artists, perhaps the most famous associated with the state is Georgia O'Keeffe. She painted objects such as flowers and animal skulls in an **abstract** way. She also painted scenes of the New Mexican landscape. The black-on-black pottery made by Santa Fe artist Maria Martinez in the early 1900s is now prized by collectors and art museums. The black-and-white photography of Ansel Adams has been popularized on posters and calendars.

The **New Mexico Museum of Art**, built in 1917, is the **oldest museum** in the state.

Started in 1962 and held every summer, The **New Mexico Arts and Crafts Fair** is the longest-running arts festival in the state.

While enjoying the Santa Fe Opera, audiences at the opera company's outdoor theater take in breathtaking views of the foothills of the Sangre de Cristo Mountains. Albuquerque's New Mexico Symphony Orchestra and groups in other cities perform classical concerts. Albuquerque is also home to the New Mexico Ballet Company.

Both the Santa Fe Playhouse and the Albuquerque Little Theater have been staging performances since the early 1900s. Actor Freddie Prinze, Jr., grew up in Albuquerque. Actress Demi Moore was born in Roswell. She moved from soap operas to films such as *St. Elmo's Fire* and *Ghost*.

New Mexico-born actress Demi Moore received a Golden Globe nomination for her role in the 1990 blockbuster movie *Ghost*.

Many organizations and schools support the advancement of music in New Mexico, including the New Mexico School for the Arts.

Founded in 1972, the Albuquerque International Balloon Fiesta originally had a modest 13 balloons. Today, it hosts hundreds of brightly colored hot-air balloons each October.

Sports and Recreation

Albuquerque hosts a hot-air balloon festival every fall. The Albuquerque International Balloon Fiesta attracts large crowds who watch hundreds of balloons floating overhead. This event is not a race, but participants do compete. Prizes are given to the balloonist who can best perform certain feats, such as landing closest to a specified spot.

Skiing is a favorite winter sport in New Mexico. Angel Fire is a top ski resort located north of Santa Fe in the Sangre de Cristo Mountains. In the winter, snowboarders and skiers are challenged to conquer the slopes or explore the trails on cross-country skis. Angel Fire offers skiing runs for beginning and advanced skiers. In the summer, the trails are open to mountain biking, hiking, and horseback riding.

The University of New Mexico's football stadium, in Albuquerque, is the **largest sports stadium in the state,** with a seating capacity for more than **39,000 fans.**

About **750,000 people** attend the **Albuquerque International Balloon Fiesta** each year.

Although New Mexico does not have teams in the major professional sports leagues, it has been home to some great professional athletes. Pittsburgh Pirates outfielder Ralph Kiner was one of the greatest sluggers in the team's history. During each of his first seven years as a Pirate, Kiner led the National League in home runs. In 1949, he had 127 runs batted-in, which was best in the league that year. His contribution to the game was officially recognized in 1975, when he was inducted into the Baseball Hall of Fame.

Taos is a popular ski destination in winter. Skiers can take advantage of nearby Wheeler Peak, the highest peak in the state.

The Unser family, from Albuquerque, has dominated auto racing for decades. Brothers Bobby and Al Unser were racers during the 1960s, 1970s, and 1980s. Bobby won the Indianapolis 500 race three times, and Al won it four times. Al's fourth win took place in 1987, when he was 48 years old. His son, Al Unser, Jr., won the Indianapolis 500 twice in the 1990s. Now, Jason Unser and Al Unser III are vying for titles.

Angel Fire Resort hosted the UCI Mountain Bike World Cup in 2005. Dirt biker Greg Minnaar, from South Africa, won the gold medal at the event.

Get To Know NEW MEXICO

Angel Fire, New Mexico, is home to the World Shovel Race Championship, held annually in the winter.

New Mexico has more than **400 ghost towns,** including Cabezon, Mogollon, and White Oaks.

The ancient 70-acre Acoma pueblo, known as Sky City, is thought to be the **oldest continuously-inhabited city** in the United States.

ABOUT 75 PERCENT OF NEW MEXICO'S ROADS ARE NOT PAVED.

NEW MEXICO GETS ABOUT 1,000 REPORTS OF UFOs PER YEAR.

At the annual Whole Enchilada Fiesta, cooks in Las Cruces use 250 pounds of corn dough to make a giant tortilla.

The forest fire prevention mascot, Smokey Bear, was invented in New Mexico.

Brain Teasers

What have you learned about New Mexico after reading this book? Test your knowledge by answering these questions. All of the information can be found in the text you just read. The answers are provided below for easy reference.

1 What is the capital of New Mexico?

2 What is New Mexico's most valuable non-fuel mineral?

3 Which national forest covers 3.3 million acres in New Mexico?

4 Which famous artist has a museum named after her in Santa Fe?

5 What Native American group built multistoried cliff dwellings in New Mexico?

6 In 1848, the U.S. acquired possession of New Mexico from which country?

7 Which Pueblo Indian village is a World Heritage Site?

8 What event is held every September and celebrates Hispanic American culture?

ANSWER KEY
1. Santa Fe 2. Copper 3. Gila National Forest 4. Georgia O'Keeffe 5. Ancestral Puebloans 6. Mexico 7. Taos Pueblo 8. The Spanish Market

Key Words

abstract: creative artwork that may not represent an object realistically

antennae: metal rods or wire devices by which radio waves are sent and received

archaeologists: scientists who study early peoples through their artifacts and remains

badlands: dry places where rapid erosion has cut strange shapes in the soil or rocks

byways: side roads

expedition: a journey for a specific purpose

irrigate: to transport water to farmland

kachinas: among the Pueblo Indians, ancestral spirits that visit the living

larvae: insect offspring in a wormlike stage

mesas: high plateaus with steep sides

phenomena: events that are considered unusual or extraordinary

proximity: nearness

reservoirs: storage areas created to collect and store water for future use

rituals: series of actions used in a religious ceremony

rustlers: cattle thieves

tributaries: rivers or streams that join a larger river

vetoes: uses political authority to reject a proposed bill or law

Index

Log on to www.av2books.com

AV² by Weigl brings you media enhanced books that support active learning. Go to www.av2books.com, and enter the special code found on page 2 of this book. You will gain access to enriched and enhanced content that supplements and complements this book. Content includes video, audio, weblinks, quizzes, a slide show, and activities.

AV² Online Navigation

Audio
Listen to sections of the book read aloud

Book Pages
AV² pages directly correspond to pages in the book.

Video
Watch informative video clips.

Key Words
Study vocabulary, and complete a matching word activity.

Embedded Weblinks
Gain additional information for research.

Try This!
Complete activities and hands-on experiments.

Quizzes
Test your knowledge.

Slide Show
View images and captions, and prepare a presentation.

AV² was built to bridge the gap between print and digital. We encourage you to tell us what you like and what you want to see in the future.

Sign up to be an AV² Ambassador at www.av2books.com/ambassador.

Due to the dynamic nature of the Internet, some of the URLs and activities provided as part of AV² by Weigl may have changed or ceased to exist. AV² by Weigl accepts no responsibility for any such changes. All media enhanced books are regularly monitored to update addresses and sites in a timely manner. Contact AV² by Weigl at 1-866-649-3445 or av2books@weigl.com with any questions, comments, or feedback.